A Mystery, Wrapped in an Enigma, Served on a Bed of Lettuce

A Collection of Cartoons by Mick Stevens

A FIRESIDE BOOK
Published by Simon & Schuster Inc.
New York   London   Toronto   Sydney   Tokyo

Fireside
Simon & Schuster Building
Rockefeller Center
1230 Avenue of the Americas
New York, New York 10020

Manufactured in the United States of America

1   3   5   7   9   10   8   6   4   2

Library of Congress Cataloging in Publication Data

Stevens, Mick.
  A mystery, wrapped in an enigma, served on a bed of lettuce : a
collection of cartoons / by Mick Stevens.
        p.   cm.
  "A Fireside book."
  1. American wit and humor, Pictorial.   I. Title.
NC1429.S645A4   1989a
741.5'973—dc20   89-34820
                                                        CIP

ISBN 0-671-65999-5

Of the 172 drawings in this collection, 74 first appeared in *The New Yorker* and were copyrighted © 1979 to 1989,
inclusive, by The New Yorker Magazine, Inc.; 13 appeared in *The National Law Journal,* copyrighted © 1987 and 1988

Continued on page 128

Introduction

I have several calls in to Mick Stevens. I need some facts in order to write this Introduction. I placed the last call about three hours ago. I'm just waiting for the facts—you know, height, weight, date and place of birth, that sort of thing. How am I supposed to write this if I don't have the relevant data? What am I supposed to do? Conjure it up out of thin air? Create a tissue of lies, a fabric of deceit, a quilt of mendacity?

Will he call? Who knows? And yet I have to press on. I'm working under a deadline here. Yes, a *deadline.* Don't shake your head in disbelief. You think just because some of us earn our keep by drawing cartoons, the black sheep of the Art family, that we don't have deadlines? Well, let's just set the record straight on that one, pal. Right now I'm dealing with the biggest deadline of them all—Tuesday.

That's right. Tuesday. Six, maybe seven P.M. Eight o'clock, tops.

Mick's editor called to say he needs this Intro right away because Simon & Schuster has suddenly decided that they actually want to print this book that you are now holding in your hands. The fact that Mick asked me to write this thing about five years ago has nothing at all to do with it and I'll tell you why. Five years ago he didn't even have a publisher, so, believe me, there was no great rush.

Right now I've got about sixteen messages backed up on his answering machine. There's a certain urgency here. I'm drinking a lot of espresso because excessive caffeine will make the wait more interesting. It will make me leap at the slightest sound and take my mind off the continuing venomous silence of the telephone. He'll be sorry if he doesn't call back soon. I'll start making up stuff. Or worse, maybe I'll just tell the truth.

I know where he is. It's a nice day. I'm stuck here by the phone, but he's out in his fancy sports car with the top down. Maybe he's got a couple of hot babes with him and maybe they'll stop at some little roadhouse where he can fuel up on a couple of those vodka-and-cokes that he seems to like so much. Or maybe if I'm lucky he'll get a sudden craving for some squid. Not a lot of people know this, but Mick is a real squid-head. His refrigerator is usually jammed full of the stuff. If I concentrate real hard, maybe I can get him to think squid—a big steaming mound of scrumptious, rubbery fried squid. Yummy! And the answering machine with all my messages is right there in the very same house with the squid!! I'm no fool!!!

He'll be calling any minute now.

But while I wait, let me tell you a story about Mick, which may or may not be true. For years he was being hassled by a female acquaintance of his who had recently become "born again." This woman apparently wanted to save Mick's soul, thereby gaining extra girl-scout points for some future appointment in heaven. She was obsessed. She kept sending him letters urging him to find Jesus. Then came a steady barrage of phone calls in which she insisted that she would help him find the Lord. "You must find Jesus," she insisted. "You will find Him." The calls became more frequent the closer it got to Christmastime. She was driving him nuts. He stopped answering the phone. More and more he'd find himself leaving his house and going for rides farther and farther into the country. One night as he drove aimlessly through the hills of northern Connecticut, he came upon a small church located at a crossroads. It was after midnight. He stopped the car, got out, and walked over to the life-size Nativity scene that had been set up under a towering pine. He found himself kneeling there beside the crib in the moonlight, staring down at the tiny plaster figure in swaddling clothes lying on its bed of straw. He put a hand out and touched it. A cold wind blew through the treetops as he bent forward and lifted the figure in his arms. It didn't weigh much. He stood and walked with it back to his car. The next day he sent the figure parcel post to his born-again friend. The enclosed note read simply: "I found Him."

That's Mick, and that's his brand of laconic, deadpan wit, the kind that sneaks up on you and knocks you right out of your chair. It's this sense of normalcy in a world gone absurd (or vice versa) that informs the very best cartoons, and Mick has evolved into one of the finest and funniest practitioners of the art that there is. But I don't have to tell you that. The proof is apparent in the pages of this book. So do yourself a favor and stop reading this stupid introduction and get on with it.

Oh, by the way, Mick Stevens was born in the town of _____ in _____. He stands _____ feet, _____ inches, and weighs in at a scale-crushing _____ pounds, buck naked.

—Jack Ziegler
Somewhere in the Litchfield Hills waiting for the phone to ring
February 1989

ROCK 'N' ROLODEX

CHILD FROM ANOTHER PLANET

ED'S LAST RIDE

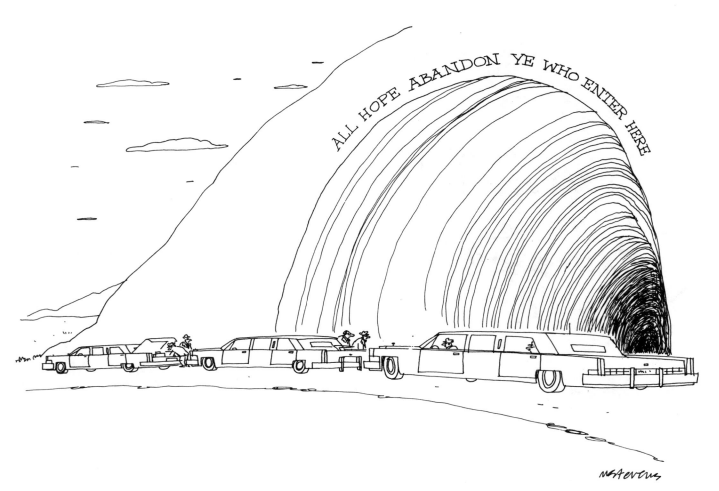

THEIR SONG

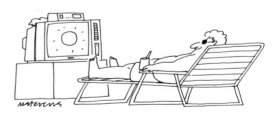

THE TANNING CHANNEL

SMOKEY THE DUCK

THE WIDE WORLD OF SPORTS

HARD TIMES FOR RL246

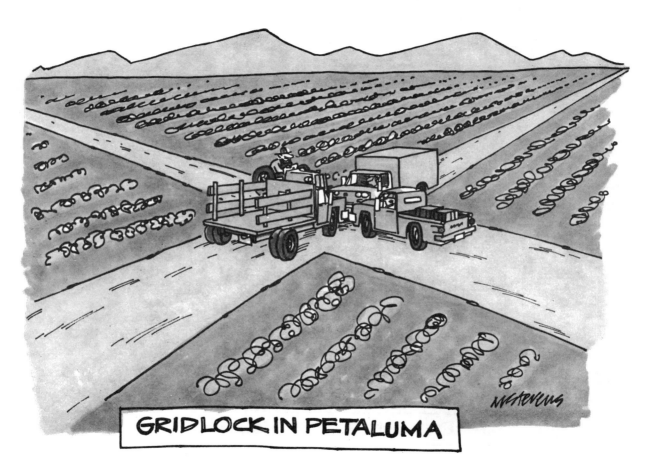

GRIDLOCK IN PETALUMA

THE LAW OF THE WEST MEETS THE LAW OF THE SEA

The Four Seasons

Spring

Summer

Fall

Cold and Flu

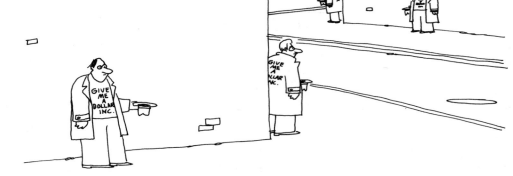

UNSOLICITED TAKEOVER OFFER

CHICKEN LITTLE

THE POTHOLE NATIONAL BANK

"Good afternoon. Kelly, Henderson & Farnsworth."

STAND-UP ATTORNEY

"Those were today's specials. Now here's a list of today's most active stocks. . . ."

| WOMEN'S WEAR LINGERIE | SHOES UMBRELLAS OFFICE SUPPLIES | TVs VCRs HOUSEHOLD APPLIANCES |

A MYSTERY, WRAPPED IN AN ENIGMA,
SERVED ON A BED OF LETTUCE.

THE MAN WHO INVENTED DENTAL FLOSS

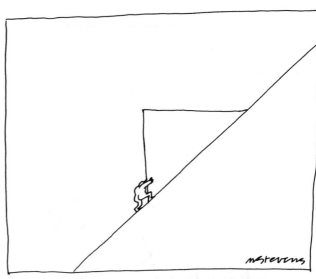

THE MYTH OF ISOSCELES

THE SPLIT-THEATRE EXPERIENCE

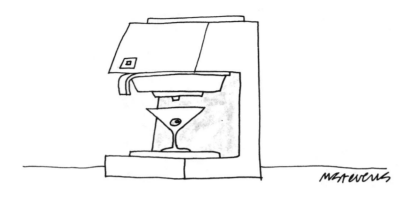

MR. MARTINI

MIGRATION STORY

THE SCHOOL OF HARD KNOCKS

ED NELSON, HUMAN TIME-BOMB

TWO APPROACHES

42

OVERNIGHT SENSATION

"Honey, I'm home."

LUNCHTIME FOR DIOGENES

Note-Crazy

THE CRITIC

PRE-COLUMBIAN COFFEE

46

DIRECTOR'S DAY OFF

OLD COMMUTERS' HOME

50

YOUR PROBLEMS

WOODY ALLEN'S PROBLEMS

THE DECAFÉ

53

"That was quite unintentional, I assure you."

SUPER BOWL MONDAY

THE MOOD REPORT

LONG-DISTANCE

MIAMI NICE

WINTER COAT

POWER - PLEADING

61

DR. JEKYL and MR. ED

CHOCOLATE LOVERS' LEAP

HEALTH AND RACKET CLUB

64

FAN

FANATIC

66

STEVE-O-LANTERN

67

"POW!"

THE ALL-COLLISION CHANNEL

COINCIDENCE OR WHAT?

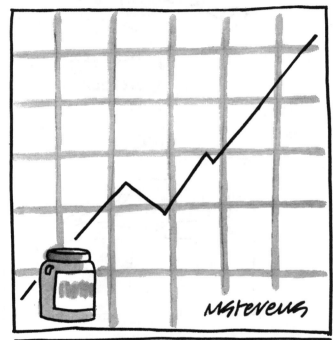

HOWARD L.'S ANXIETY LEVEL

THE PRICE OF PEANUT BUTTER

THE LIFE OF BACH, AS DIRECTED BY SAM PECKINPAH

LONG AFTER OFFICE-HOURS, HARRY'S SCOWL
REMAINED AT HIS DESK

MAN WHO HAS GIVEN UP ALL HIS BAD HABITS

THE INSOMNIAC

ROGET'S BRONTOSAURUS

THE 4th OF FEBRUARY

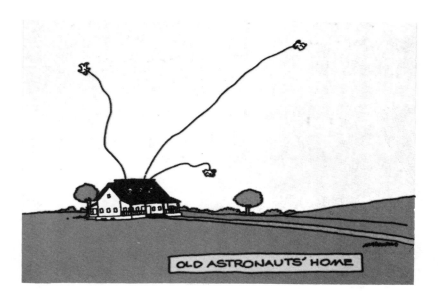

THE NO-BOOK-OF-THE-MONTH CLUB

JUGGLING FOR FITNESS

"Ouch! . . . I mean, nice to meet you. . . ."

NEW, IMPROVED CAT

DIET FOR A LARGE PLANET

MEGARONI

ULTRA-BITS

SUPERSNAX

FETTUCINI AL GROSSO

OFF-SEASON

WHAT SANTA'S REINDEER
DO THE REST OF THE YEAR

DASHER

PROPRIETOR OF A FAST-FOOD FRANCHISE

DANCER

DOING STAND-UP COMEDY

VIXEN

INVOLVED WITH AN OBSCURE RELIGIOUS CULT ON THE WEST COAST

PRANCER

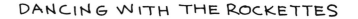

DANCING WITH THE ROCKETTES

COMET

SELLING REAL ESTATE

CUPID

LEARNING TO PLAY THE CLARINET

BLITZEN

WEATHER-DEER, CHANNEL SIX

DONDER

ON THE GRAND PRIX CIRCUIT

RUDOLPH

AT EDDIE'S DEW DROP INN

"Hey! The sky is falling! Am I right or am I wrong?!"

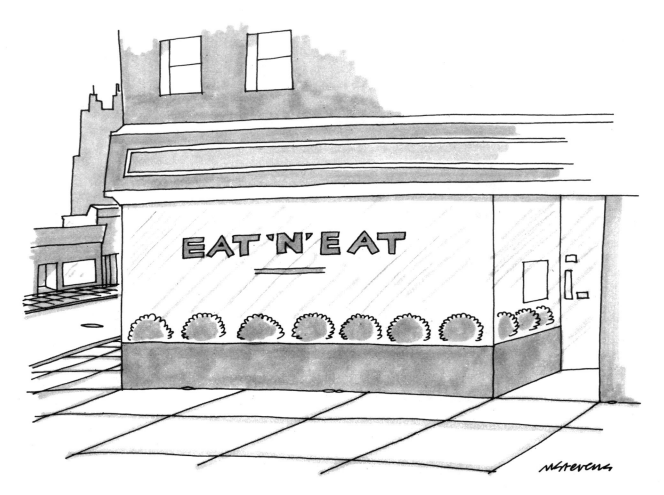

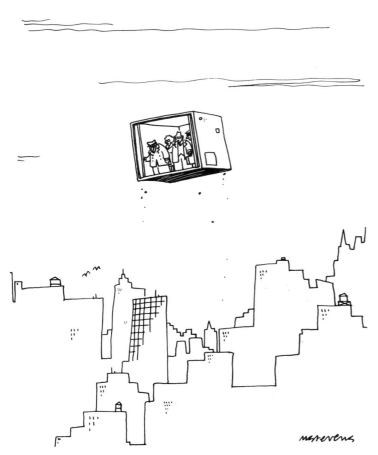

"Thirtieth floor . . . oops! Sorry, folks, my mistake!"

SNOWMAN FROM ANOTHER PLANET

89

A CASE OF AGGRAVATED INSECTICIDE

ANOTHER SNOWMAN TRAGEDY

94

"Well, Bob, this is kind of a big day for you, isn't it?"

BEGINNERS' SLOPE

THE EVOLUTION OF THE DUTCH DOOR

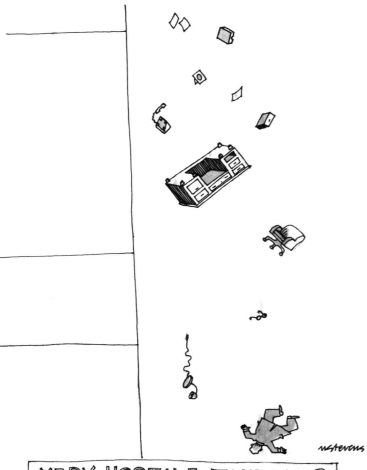

VERY HOSTILE TAKEOVER

SO THIS IS NEW HAVEN...

ARMCHAIR TRAVELER

SUSHI FOR TOUGH GUYS

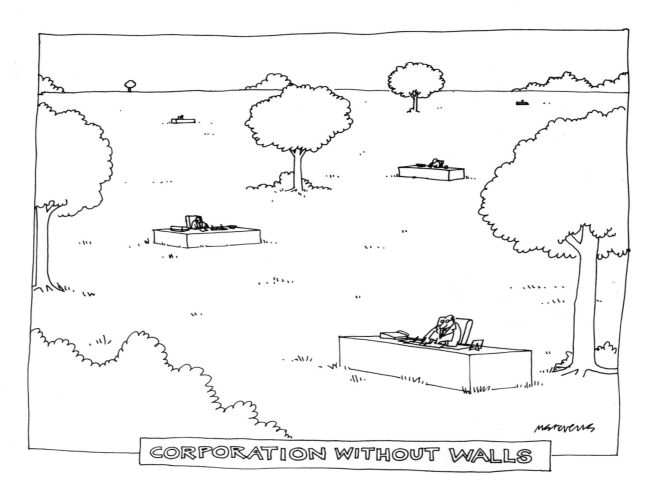

CORPORATION WITHOUT WALLS

LIBERTY INVITING A COUPLE OF GUYS TO LUNCH

EXECUTIVE FITNESS PLAN

EGGS BENEDICT ARNOLD

SWISS ARMY COUCH

109

"It's me, sweetheart—the madman you married in 1946."

113

FREE-FLOATING ANXIETY
(MAGNIFIED 200,000,000 TIMES)

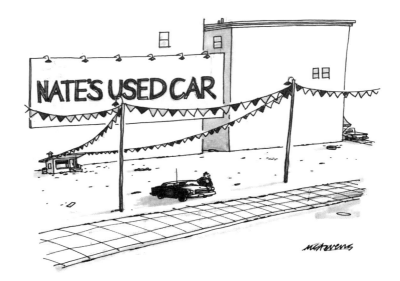

"Oops! My floor, guys. I'll see you later."

HURRICANE WILLY

WHITE-COLLAR MISDEMEANOR

Ceci n'est pas un Magritte

NOISE PRISON

"Now, you wait right here while I go ask my wife for a divorce."

PAWN   KNIGHT BISHOP ROOK ATTORNEY QUEEN KING

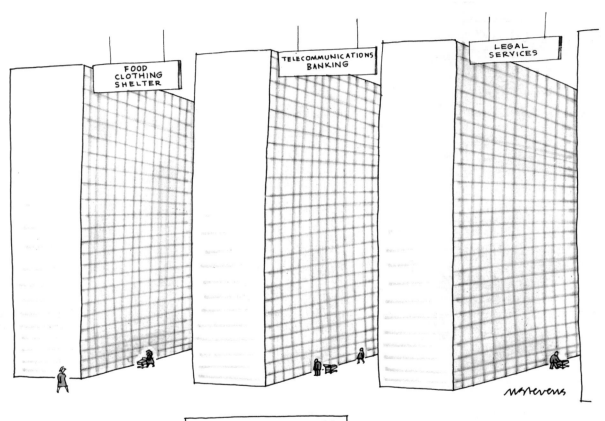

MEGA-MARKETING

ALLEGRO CON EDDIE

PEAK

OFF-PEAK

127